BUG
ON A BIKE

CHRIS MONROE

CAROLRHODA BOOKS   MINNEAPOLIS

To Alex —CM

Carolrhoda Books
A division of Lerner Publishing Group, Inc.
241 First Avenue North
Minneapolis, MN 55401 USA

For reading levels and more information, look up this title at
www.lernerbooks.com.

Main body text set in Gomorrah Regular 20/24
Typeface provided by Chank.

Library of Congress Cataloging-in-Publication Data

Monroe, Chris, author, illustrator.
    Bug on a bike / written and illustrated by Chris Monroe.
      pages   cm
    Summary: "The bug on a bike is riding somewhere, but no one quite knows
the destination. But that doesn't stop all the other animals from following
along"— provided by publisher.
    ISBN 978-1-4677-2154-7 (lib. bdg. : alk. paper)
    ISBN 978-1-4677-4622-9 (eBook)
    [1. Stories in rhyme. 2. Bicycles and bicycling—Fiction. 3. Birthdays—Fiction.
4. Parties—Fiction. 5. Insects—Fiction. 6. Animals—Fiction.] I. Title.
PZ8.3.M756Bu 2014
[E]—dc23   2013048153

Manufactured in the United States of America
1 – DP – 7/15/14

Mike was at home.
He was baking some pies.

So off the two went.
They rolled down the dirt road
and stopped by the swamp
to find Randy the Toad.

Randy was fishing.

Randy looked puzzled.
He took off his slippers.
He sat on a mushroom
and packed up some kippers.

So Randy the Toad
and a lizard named Mike

rolled down the road
with the bug on a bike.

Soon they were joined by some ants on a log,

Butterfly Andy,

and the polka dot dog.

An athletic pickle was
lifting some weights,

and a scruffy orange cat
was tying his skates.

They all came along.
It's as simple as that!

They were
joined by a
nickel

and a chimp
in a hat.

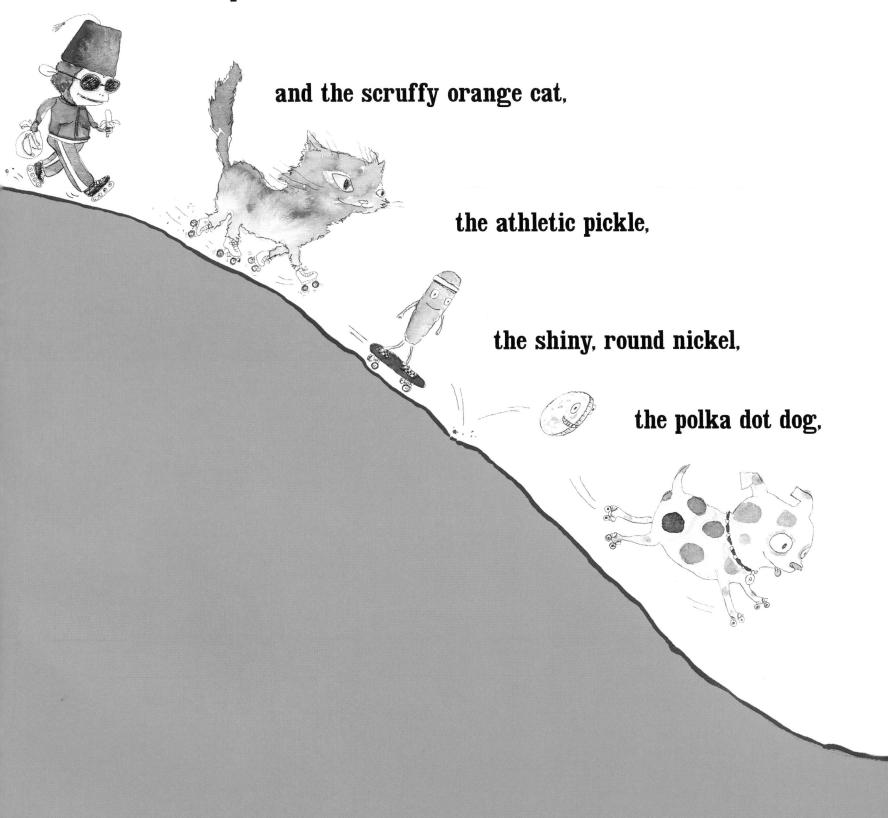

So the chimp in a hat

and the scruffy orange cat,

the athletic pickle,

the shiny, round nickel,

the polka dot dog,

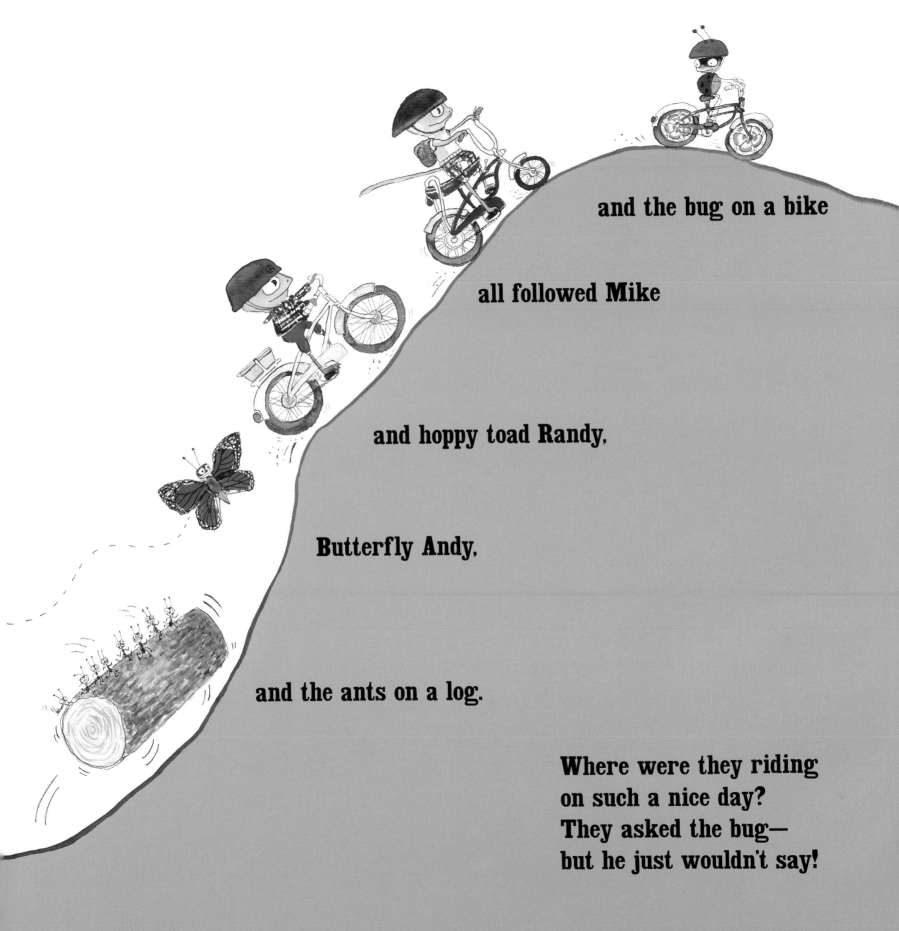

and the bug on a bike

all followed Mike

and hoppy toad Randy,

Butterfly Andy,

and the ants on a log.

Where were they riding
on such a nice day?
They asked the bug—
but he just wouldn't say!

They found Skater **Bunny**
and a bear with some honey.

They invited a mouse
and a snake in a blouse.

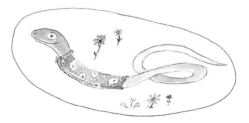

They were wondering where
they were going out there!
The bug wouldn't say.
It didn't seem fair!

Where were they going?
They just could not see.
Where was this place
they were going to be?

Then they stopped
by the meadow
to pick up the herd

and rode up to a tree
to collect a red bird.

They soon gathered up
the three wild billy goats

and some carpenter clams
building wheels for their boats.

So the clams in their boats
and the three billy goats,
the flying red bird,
the thundering herd,
the snake in her blouse,
the little gray mouse,
the bear and his honey,
the skateboarding bunny,
the chimp in the hat,

the scruffy orange cat,
the athletic pickle,
the shiny, round nickel,
the polka dot dog,
the ants on the log,
and Butterfly Andy
with hoppy toad Randy . . .

all followed Mike
and the bug on a bike!

They rode past some boulders
along a steep trail.
They crossed a small river.
They rode on a rail.

ABANDONED
TRACKS

They wound through the forest.
It seemed like a mile!

So the clams and their boats
and the three billy goats
ate buckets of nachos
and chugged root beer floats.

The happy red bird
and the fast, hungry herd
headed straight for the cake
without saying a word.

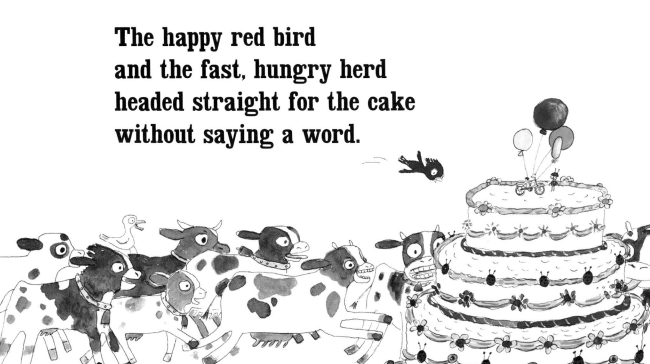

And the snake in her blouse,
with the cake-eating mouse
drank blue bubble tea
in a blue bouncy house.

And the bunny was cool—
wasn't breaking a rule—
when he told sticky bear
to clean up in the pool!

Then the chimp in the hat
and the ketchupy cat
tried to break the piñata
with a bubblegum bat.

Then the break-dancing pickle
started busting a move,
and the gymnastic nickel
got into a groove.

And the polka dot dog
licked the pickle (he's dill).
And the ants on a log
rolled their timber downhill!

Then Butterfly Andy
and hoppy toad Randy
played banjos and sang
and shared five bowls of candy.

While Mike was quite helpful,
he handed out toys—
light-up trinkets and gizmos
that made lots of noise.

So all of the friends
did the things that they like,
enjoying the birthday
of the bug on a bike.

And the bug on a bike?
Well, he just had a ball.
Seeing all his friends happy
was the most fun of all.

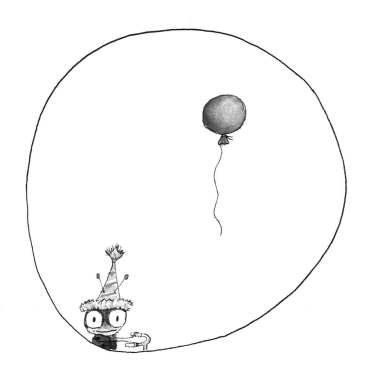

The End